oo V

w Oo

v Z

z W

ng Ng

Zainab and Viv sit on swings.

1

Look!

Zainab swings up and jumps off.

Viv swings up...

...twists and slips!

Viv's foot is red and sore.

At hospital, Viv, Zainab and Dad
wait in a waiting room.

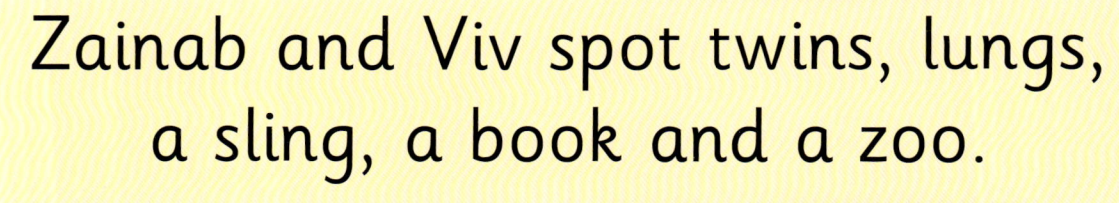

Zainab and Viv spot twins, lungs, a sling, a book and a zoo.

In Room Seven,
Doctor Bloom looks at Viv's foot.

Doctor Bloom dresses Viv's foot.